visit us at www.abdopublishing.com

Reinforced library bound edition published in 2009 by Spotlight, a division of ABDO Publishing Group, 8000 West 78th Street, Edina, Minnesota 55439. This edition reprinted by arrangement with TOKYOPOP Inc. www.tokyopop.com

Written by	Joshua Elder
Illustrated by	Erich Owen
Retouch and Lettering	Alyson Stetz
Cover Design	Chris Tjaslma
Editor	Rob Valois
Digital Imaging Manager	Chris Buford

Library of Congress Cataloging-in-Publication Data

Elder, Joshua.
  Mail order ninja / written by Joshua Elder ; illustrated by Erich Owen. -- Reinforced library bound ed.
    v. cm.
  Summary: Presents two previously published manga volumes in which timid Indiana fifth-grader Timmy McAllister obtains his very own ninja to face the bullies and snobs of L. Frank Baum Elementary School.
  Contents: Mail order ninja -- Timmy strikes back.
  ISBN 978-1-59961-568-4 (vol. 1: Mail order ninja)
  1. Graphic novels. [1. Graphic novels. 2. Ninja--Fiction. 3. Schools--Fiction. 4. Bullies--Fiction.] I. Owen, Erich, ill. II. Title.
  PZ7.7.E32Mai 2008
  [Fic]--dc22   2008002196

VOL. 1

WRITTEN BY JOSHUA ELDER
ILLUSTRATED BY ERICH OWEN

HAMBURG // LONDON // LOS ANGELES // TOKYO

nin ja (nin′ jə) *n*., *pl*. **-ja** or **-jas**
Any of a class of elite feudal Japanese warriors trained in the arts of stealth and espionage: "The ninja looked quite fetching in his black ensemble."
-adj. [slang] very good, pleasing, excellent: "Dude, this floral arrangement is totally ninja!"

BIO

NAME: Felicity's Entourage
OCCUPATION: Hangers-on
FAVORITE PERSON: Who do you think?

CHOP

CUT

ZWISSH

KRAK

THUD

BIO

NAME: Yoshida Jiro
OCCUPATION: Legendary ninja warrior
FUN FACT: Jiro once had a promising music career and was dubbed the "Japanese Barry Manilow" by critics.

Ninja walk alone.
Shadows are the only ones
That walk beside them.

-ancient ninja proverb

Chapter 2

WE NOW RETURN YOU
TO YOUR REGULARLY
SCHEDULED
GRAPHIC NOVEL
ALREADY IN PROGRESS.

Chapter 3

YAAAAAH!!!!

KRASH

HE'S *RUINED* IT! HE'S RUINED *EVERYTHING!*

BIO

NAME: Stately Huntington Manor
OCCUPATION: Foreboding villainous lair
OF ROOMS: 137
Highlights include a sauna, an indoor
golf course, and a working medieval
dungeon.

SILENT BUT DEADLY

Everyone knows that ninja are awesome. But some ninja are more awesomer than others. And the ninja of Clan Yoshida are the awesomest of all. This is their story in all its awesomity.

BY CHARLES EASTMAN-LAIRD

.....

It was a balmy Autumn day in 1974 when I had my first encounter with a ninja. I was a sixth-year student at the Wackford Squeers School for Boys in Sussex, and my class had gone on a field trip to the Tower of London. As fate would have it, the evil shinobi Hakuryuu Katashi chose that same day to attempt a theft of the most valuable collection of shiny trinkets and baubles in existence: the Crown Jewels of England. Which, as every Englishman knows, are kept in the Tower's Jewel House where they're watched over day and night by the ever-vigilant Tower Guard.

Yet such was Katashi's skill at thievery that he was able to nick the Jewels without the guards even noticing they were gone. Disguised as an Arab potentate, Katashi planned to make his escape via the front gate as if he were just another tourist. And he would have gotten away with it too if it weren't for Yoshida Daisuke and his American blood brother Tarantino Jones, who is famous for being the only samurai to ever sport an afro.

The two warriors were in town to play Rosencrantz and Guildenstern in the Royal Shakespeare Company's famous production of *Hamlet* when Daisuke had a fearful premonition that bade him journey to the Tower.

It was there that he found his old enemy Katashi in the midst of an almost-successful getaway. Daisuke's ninja senses allowed him to see through the thieving shinobi's disguise, leaving Katashi no choice but to try and fight his way to freedom. Katashi was the White Dragon Clan's most skilled warrior, but he knew he was no match for both Daisuke and Tarantino. So he did what White Dragon ninja always do: he cheated. At Katashi's command, a dozen Clan Hakuryuu warriors appeared from out of out thin air in their trademark clouds of white smoke. The battle was joined.

Daisuke and Tarantino emerged

忍者

NINJA

triumphant, of course. The Crown Jewels were recovered and Katashi fell to his death from the top of London Bridge. Actually, he didn't all-the-way die. He just sort of died and then got better as evil ninja are wont to do. Still, it was a resounding victory for the forces of good, one that I got to witness firsthand. Afterwards, the two victorious heroes signed autographs for me and my classmates and gave us all free passes to their show. It was the greatest day of my young life.

As a rule, ninja don't act this way. They prefer to retreat back into the shadows once their job is done. Not the Yoshida. They may be ninja, but they also know how to party. This dichotomy – silent and serene one minute, fun-loving and flamboyant the next – has made Clan Yoshida the most famous and beloved ninja clan in the world. Though this wasn't always the case.

Long before they were ninja, the revered Yoshida ancestors were simple farmers. Hence the name Yoshida, which literally means "good field." A kindhearted and generous people, the Yoshida lived peaceful lives tucked away in the mountainous Iga province of ancient Japan. They would tend their crops during the day, and at night they would entertain each other through painting, calligraphy, theater, poetry and music. The cultivation of artistic talent has remained a cornerstone of Clan Yoshida training to this day, a way of balancing the scales of karma. For as the old Yoshida proverb says, "History judges a man by what he creates, not by what he destroys. Unless he should also destroy all the historians. Then history won't judge him at all."

Speaking of history, it was nearly 1,000 years ago that the Yoshida Clan made the transition from farmers to ninja warriors. A great army that rode under the banner of a White Dragon was sweeping across the land, destroying all in its path. Its legions numbered in the tens of thousands and its generals wielded powerful magic that made them nigh-invincible on the field of battle. Rather than meet such a formidable enemy head-on, the various tribes and peoples of the Iga province abandoned their villages to hide in the surrounding forest. From there they waged a guerilla campaign against the White Dragon army, but they lacked the skills or the numbers to be anything more than a minor annoyance – the military equivalent of a pebble in one's shoe.

Enter the *tengu,* wily forest spirits that had been driven to near extinction by the White Dragons. They taught the men of Iga the basic principles of what would come to be known as *ninjutsu,* the art of going unseen. With these new skills at their disposal, the men of Iga – led by the warriors of Clan Yoshida – dealt a devastating defeat to the White Dragons. Their power broken, the Dragons had to adopt the methods of their enemies and become a ninja clan in their own right. This led to a lucrative second career for the Dragons as international mercenaries, selling their talents to the highest bidder in order to finance their own plans for world domination. And just like before, the only ones capable of standing in their way were the shinobi of Clan Yoshida.

Thus began an epic blood feud that has lasted the better part of a millennium. Over the centuries the clans have fought on all seven continents, beneath the sea in the lost city of Atlantis, and even on the surface of the moon where a Yoshida ninja prevented the assassination of Neil Armstrong and Buzz Aldrin by a White Dragon agent in the employ of the Soviet Union. Yet for all their sound and fury, the battles signified nothing. The clans were locked in an eternal stalemate – yin forever balanced by yang. A long twilight struggle with no end in sight, etc., etc. Then a new variable was introduced that completely changed the equation: a variable named Yoshida Jiro.

Driven by revenge, Jiro almost single-handedly reduced the entire Hakuryuu organization to a shadow of its former self and then slew the clan *jounin* (literally "high ninja") Nobunaga – who as of this writing remains dead – in single combat. His thirst for vengeance quenched, Jiro soon realized how meaningless his life had become. He had lost everything that he ever truly cared about and had become an empty vessel filled with nothing but rage. He wanted to learn how to love once again – to have fun once again.

So he sold himself into indentured servitude to a random American child as part of a promotional contest for the inaugural issue of the Jacques Co. toy catalog. It was an unorthodox approach to say the least, but that's just how Jiro rolls. For his sake, and for the sake of Clan Yoshida, I pray he succeeds.

ABOUT THE AUTHOR:
Charles Eastman-Laird is a distinguished Professor of Ninjology at Oxford University and the author of *Ninjas: Quite Possibly the Coolest Thing Ever* (Completely Fake Press) from which this article is adapted.

MAIL ORDER NINJA

VOL. 2 PREVIEW

NOW THAT FELICITY HAS HER OWN *EVIL* MAIL ORDER NINJA--ACTUALLY, SHE HAS MORE LIKE 100 OF THEM--LIFE IN CHERRY CREEK IS ABOUT TO GET A LOT MORE...INTERESTING. BECAUSE FELICITY DOESN'T JUST WANT REVENGE ON OUR INTREPID HEROES, SHE WANTS TO ENSLAVE THE ENTIRE FREAKIN' TOWN. AND WHEN JIRO FALLS IN BATTLE, TIMMY MUST FIND THE COURAGE TO STAND ALONE AGAINST THE FORCES OF EVIL AND UNCOOLNESS.

SO GET READY FOR A WHOLE NEW LEVEL OF OFF-THE-HOOK NINJA ACTION AND OFF-THE-WALL NINJA COMEDY IN THE NEXT PULSE-POUNDING, SENSES-SHATTERING, SIDE-SPLITTING CHAPTER IN THE *MAIL ORDER NINJA* SAGA...
TIMMY STRIKES BACK!

DATE DUE

BRODART, CO.

Cat. No. 23-221-003